An I Can Read Book™

# Minnie and Moo
# Will You Be
# My Valentine?

## Den s
## Cazet

HarperCollins Publishers

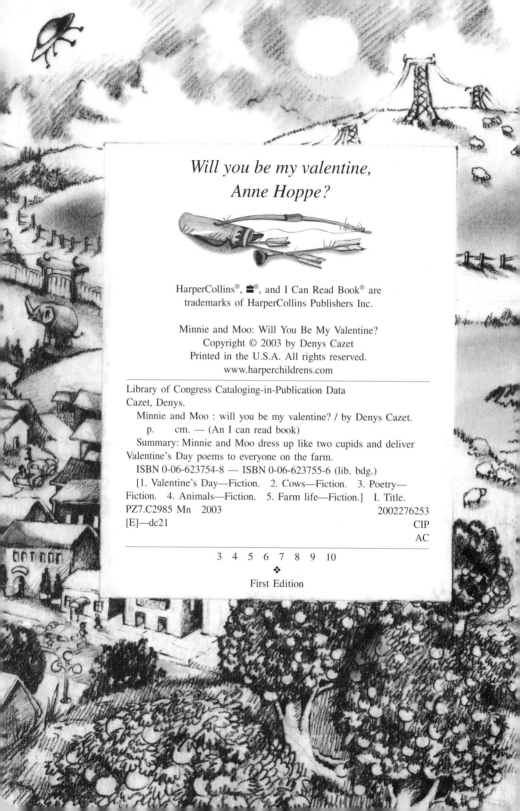

*Will you be my valentine,*
*Anne Hoppe?*

HarperCollins®, ▟®, and I Can Read Book® are
trademarks of HarperCollins Publishers Inc.

Minnie and Moo: Will You Be My Valentine?
Copyright © 2003 by Denys Cazet
Printed in the U.S.A. All rights reserved.
www.harperchildrens.com

Library of Congress Cataloging-in-Publication Data
Cazet, Denys.
  Minnie and Moo : will you be my valentine? / by Denys Cazet.
     p.    cm. — (An I can read book)
  Summary: Minnie and Moo dress up like two cupids and deliver
Valentine's Day poems to everyone on the farm.
  ISBN 0-06-623754-8 — ISBN 0-06-623755-6 (lib. bdg.)
  [1. Valentine's Day—Fiction.   2. Cows—Fiction.   3. Poetry—
Fiction.   4. Animals—Fiction.   5. Farm life—Fiction.]   I. Title.
PZ7.C2985 Mn   2003                              2002276253
[E]—dc21                                                      CIP
                                                                AC

           3   4   5   6   7   8   9   10
                          ❖
                  First Edition

# Sweet Love

Minnie and Moo

sat under the old oak tree.

A box of cream puffs

sat on Minnie's lap.

"Since I'm on a diet," she said,

"I'll start with the smallest."

Suddenly, Moo sang out,

"SWEET LOOOOOOOVE!"

"OH!" Minnie cried.

The cream puff fell into the grass.

"Love is everywhere!" said Moo.

"So is my cream puff!" said Minnie.

"Sorry," said Moo. "I was just—"

"Reading!" said Minnie. "I saw you!"

"Reading love poems." Moo sighed.

"Humph," said Minnie.

Moo picked up the cream puff.

"I have a poem for you, Minnie.

I made it up myself."

Moo told Minnie

her poem.

### Ode to the Cream Puff

*Your peaks are crowned*

*with the sweetest snow;*

*Your valleys crisp*

*in deep-fried dough;*

*Your insides filled*

*with that custard stuff;*

*How I love thee,*

*my sweet Cream Puff.*

Minnie burst into tears.

"That was so beautiful!"

Moo dabbed Minnie's eyes

with a hanky.

"I didn't mean to make you cry."

"It's not your fault," Minnie sniffed.

"Poems about food make me weep."

# Cupids to Go

Minnie dried her eyes.

"You should be more careful

where you aim a poem," she said.

Moo smiled. "It's Valentine's Day."

Minnie pointed at the old apple tree.

"Tell that to the dog," said Minnie.

"See? He's barking at the cat again."

The dog barked. The cat hissed.

"Maybe you should aim a love poem

at them," said Minnie.

"They could use it."

"That's a wonderful idea!" said Moo.

"What?"

"Love poems for the needy!" said Moo.

"But, Moo—"

Moo raised her arms toward the sky.

"Cupids to Go. Minnie and Moo's
Love Poem Service. We Deliver!"

"But, Moo—"

"We'll need two pairs of tights,

two tutus, wings, a bow, and arrows,"

said Moo. "They're in the barn."

"But, Moo—"

"I'll write the love poems," said Moo.

# Chickens in Love

Minnie opened a big box.

"I found everything," she said.

Minnie and Moo dressed quickly.

Minnie picked up the bow and arrows.

Moo stuffed her poems into a bag.

"Let's start with the chickens,"
she said.

They tiptoed to the chicken coop.

Moo tied a poem to an arrow.

Minnie shot it into the chicken yard.

"Oh!" cried the chickens.

One of the chickens looked at the note.

"Why . . . it's a love note!" she said.

"From who?" asked another.

"Oh, my!" gasped the chicken.

"It's from the peacock!"

She read the poem out loud.

*You are the valentine*

*my heart must seek.*

*Let's dance in the moonlight*

*beak to beak.*

*I've got the music,*

*you've got the legs—*

*don't let me forget*

*to pick up some eggs.*

*All my love,*

*The Peacock*

The chickens swooned.

Elvis, the rooster,

stepped out of the coop.

"Hey, girls! Where's my lunch?"

Moo tied a poem to another arrow.

"This is for the rooster," she said.

Minnie aimed the arrow.

SMACK!

It stuck to the door of the coop.

Elvis looked at the arrow.

He looked at the chickens.

"Geez," he said.

"I'll make my own lunch."

# Love Gets Mixed Up

Minnie looked down the road.

"Moo, the Holsteins are coming!"

"I have one for them, too," said Moo.

"It's in my bag somewhere."

"Hurry," Minnie whispered.

"I think this is it," said Moo.

She tied the poem to an arrow.

"Shoot!" Moo said.

The arrow flew down the road.

SMACK!

"HEY!" cried Bea.

Madge pulled it off.

"It's a valentine poem," she said.

"It must be for me." Bea giggled.

Bea read the poem.

*Dearest buffalo lips,*

*your ultra-wide hips*

*are as big as six ships.*

*So what can I say*

*but "anchors away!"*

*Have a wonderful,*

   *wonderful,*

      *Valentine's Day.*

23

Bea handed Madge the poem.

"It's for you," she said.

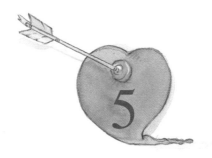

# Love, Love, Everywhere

Minnie and Moo hid behind the barn.

"This time," Minnie whispered,

"make sure it's the *right* poem."

Moo looked in her bag.

"Here's one," she said.

"Read it first!" said Minnie.

Moo read the poem.

### My Darling Ducky

*Oh, lovely ducky,*

*Miss Shovel Beak,*

*my heart will sink*

*if you spring a leak.*

"That's for the ducks," said Moo.

Minnie shot the arrow into the pond.

Moo read another.

*My love for you has never been keener,*

*my little piggy, my hot dog wiener.*

*My little piggy, don't get flustered,*

*I love you truly, with a little mustard.*

"That's for the pigs," said Moo.

Minnie shot the arrow into the pigsty.

Moo read another.

**_Love Is a Wool Sweater_**

_No need for a zipper,_

_No need for a button,_

_When you sprout_

_your own sweater_

_Around your own mutton._

"That's for the sheep," said Moo.

Minnie aimed.

When the sheep saw the arrow,

they held up their arms.

"Why are they doing that?"

Minnie asked.

"Beats me," said Moo.

Minnie shot the arrow

into the meadow.

"Any more?" asked Minnie.

"Of course," said Moo.

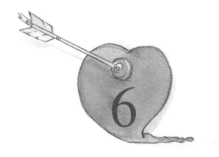

# Don Juan in Love

Don Juan del Toro

stood at the edge of the pasture,

picking his teeth.

"What a beautiful day." He sighed.

"So calm, so peaceful."

Moo tied a poem to an arrow.

Minnie aimed.

SMACK!

"Right in the kisser!"

said Minnie.

Don Juan del Toro

spit out his toothpick.

He pulled the arrow off his nose.

32

He read the poem.

*Hey, good lookin',*

*How about a kiss?*

*Aim for my lips*

*And you can't miss.*

*One for the money,*

*Two for the show,*

*Pucker up, baby,*

*I'm ready to go.*

*Will you be my valentine?*

Don Juan snorted.

He looked around the pasture.

He saw Madge and Bea

looking at a piece of paper.

Don Juan waved at the Holsteins.

"Here I come, lover lips!"

he shouted.

"See?" said Moo. "Isn't love grand?"

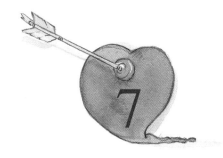

# Love in the Wash

Zeke and Zack snoozed in the sun.

Minnie aimed.

SMACK!

The turkeys woke up.

They looked at the arrow.

"INDIANS!" they shouted.

They ran through the farmer's yard.

The farmer was painting the fence.

Millie, the farmer's wife,

was hanging out the wash.

"Gracious me!" said Millie.

"Now's our chance," said Minnie.

"Find one for the farmer's wife."

Moo looked in her bag.

"They're all mixed up!" she said.

"Hurry," said Minnie.

Moo tied a poem to an arrow.

Minnie aimed.

SMACK!

"Gracious!" cried Millie.

She untied the piece of paper.

She read the poem.

### Dear Turkey Legs

*I love the way you wobble*

   *when you waddle*

   *when you walk.*

*I love the way you gobble*

   *when you waddle*

   *when you talk.*

*Will you be my valentine?*

Millie stuffed the poem into her apron.

She marched toward the farmer.

"I think she likes it," said Moo.

Moo tied another poem to an arrow.

Minnie aimed it at the farmer.

SMACK!

"Now what?" said the farmer.

He read the poem.

## Waiting for My Valentine

*Alone, I float*

*Upon the empty sea,*

*Waiting, waiting,*

*Have you forgotten me?*

*Where's my hero?*

*Where's the boat?*

*I'm tired of waiting,*

*You old goat!*

Millie glared at the farmer.

The farmer glared at Millie.

Millie pointed at her legs.

"Do these look like turkey legs?"

The farmer pointed at himself.

"Do I look like an old goat?"

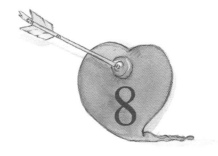

# Love Rests

The farmer looked at Millie's note.

"Millie, I didn't write this.

And look, someone sent me a note!"

"It's the same handwriting!"

said Millie.

"So . . . who wrote them?"

The farmer looked at the hill.

"Those two cows—"

"Oh, John," said Millie gently.

"Cows don't write poems."

Millie took the farmer's hand.

She led him into the house.

"I'll make some iced tea," she said.

She closed the door softly.

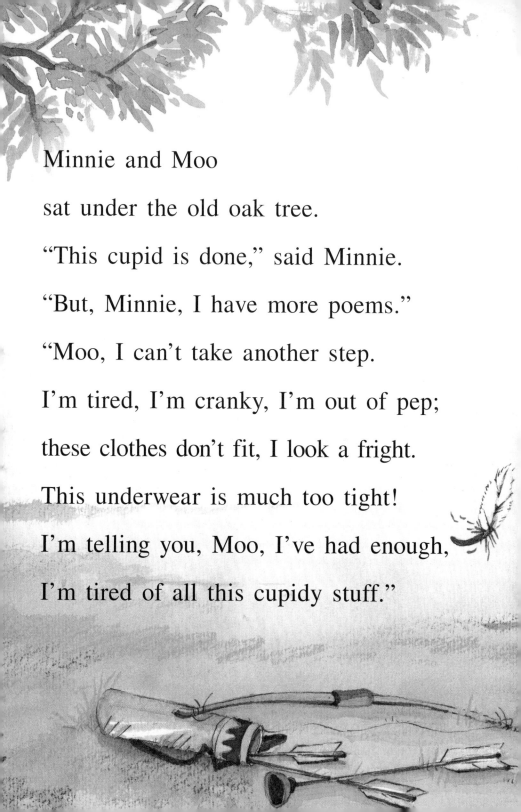

Minnie and Moo

sat under the old oak tree.

"This cupid is done," said Minnie.

"But, Minnie, I have more poems."

"Moo, I can't take another step.

I'm tired, I'm cranky, I'm out of pep;

these clothes don't fit, I look a fright.

This underwear is much too tight!

I'm telling you, Moo, I've had enough,

I'm tired of all this cupidy stuff."

"Minnie! That was a poem!"

"It was?" said Minnie.

Moo put her arm around Minnie.

"Happy Valentine's Day," she said.

"Happy Valentine's Day," said Minnie.